Do you have all the Little Red Robin books?

- [ ] Buster's Big Surprise
- [ ] The Purple Butterfly
- [ ] How Bobby Got His Pet
- [ ] When the Tooth Fairy Forgot
- [ ] Silly Name for a Monster
- [ ] The Fleas Who Fight Crime
- [ ] We Are Super!
- [ ] New Friends
- [ ] Robo-Robbie
- [ ] A Friend for Dragon
- [ ] Princess Pip's Perfect Party

Also available as ebooks

Little Red
Robin

Princess Pip's Perfect Party

Lou Kuenzler

Illustrated by Dan Crisp

■SCHOLASTIC

Scholastic Children's Books
An imprint of Scholastic Ltd
Euston House, 24 Eversholt Street
London, NW1 1DB, UK
Registered office: Westfield Road, Southam, Warwickshire, CV47 0RA
SCHOLASTIC and associated logos are trademarks and/or registered
trademarks of Scholastic Inc.

First published in the UK by Scholastic Ltd, 2014

Text copyright © Lou Kuenzler, 2014
Illustration copyright © Dan Crisp, 2014
The rights of Lou Kuenzler and Dan Crisp
to be identified as the author and illustrator of
this work have been asserted by them.

ISBN 978 1407 13909 8

Printed in China.

1 3 5 7 9 10 8 6 4 2

www.scholastic.co.uk

Chapter One

Once upon a time in a cold, snowy place called Cragland there was a little princess named Pip.

Normally, Princess Pip was a happy, smiley sort of princess with dimples in her cheeks.

But this morning Pip did not have dimples.
She had a big cross frown on her face. She was in
a very bad mood.

Pip peered out over the castle wall. Far below, she could see the royal carriage rattling away down the snowy mountain road. Pip's big sister, Princess Grace, was leaning out of the carriage and waving.

Grace was off to spend her first term at princess school. She was going to learn how to be a perfect princess, just like the ones Pip loved to look at in her favourite storybooks.

"It's not fair," wailed Pip. "I want to go to princess school, too."

Grace was going to learn to dance like a
ballerina.

"I want to dance like a ballerina!" said Pip.

But there were no ballerinas in Cragland. Just the king and his big hairy warriors.

Grace was going to learn to ride a unicorn.
"I want to ride a unicorn," said Pip.

But there were no unicorns in Cragland either.
Just big hairy yaks.

"Poo," sniffed Pip.

She could smell the big stinky muck heap behind the yak stables. She had never seen a stinky muck heap in any of her perfect princess storybooks.

Not ever!

"I'll never learn to be a proper perfect princess here," muttered Pip crossly.

"Cheer up," said the king, standing above her like an enormous bear. "You can go to princess school too . . . just as soon as you are old enough."

"But I want to go NOW," wailed Pip.

Gogo the wise old hermit poked his head out of the hay barn where he was having a nap.

"What's all this fuss?" he yawned. Gogo was the cleverest person in the whole castle.

"Papa says I can't go to princess school until I'm older," said Pip. "But that will take ages, won't it?"

"You cannot get older until you have a birthday," said Gogo wisely. Then he closed his eyes and went straight back to sleep.

"A birthday?" Now Pip smiled at last. "How perfect!" she grinned.

Chapter Two

"Papa says I can go to princess school when I'm older," thought Pip. "And Gogo says the only way to be older is to have a birthday. But I just had a birthday last month…"

Then she clapped her hands.

"What if I had an extra birthday?" she thought.
"Surely that would make me old enough to go to
princess school? I'll have a party – a proper perfect
princess birthday party!"

Pip flicked through her storybooks. There were plenty of pictures of perfect princess parties. There were birthday cakes with pink icing and pink candles...and pink party invitations with pink balloons. The princesses always arrived at their parties on unicorns and everyone wore frilly dresses (they were pink, of course).

"I'd better get started," said Pip.

"A birthday cake?" Canker the cook stirred something lumpy in his big iron cauldron. "How about a bowl of this lovely yak's milk porridge instead?"

"No!" cried Pip. "It has to be a cake, with candles for me to blow out. Please can you bake me a perfect pretty princess cake . . . with pink icing?"

"Pink icing?" Canker looked as if he was going to faint.

But Pip had hurried away.

23

Next, she had to make some proper perfect party invitations.

Chapter Three

Pip skipped across the snowy courtyard with a
bag full of party invitations. Plans for her perfect
party were going very well! Soon everyone would
know she was old enough to go to princess school.

"Hello," Pip called to Haggle, the enormous hairy herdsman. "This is for you," she said, waving a pretty pink party invitation in the air.

"Well I never." Haggle grinned proudly. "Thank you very much. I don't think I've ever been invited to a princess party before."

You are invited to Princess Pip's
Perfect Party. . .
Where she will become a whole
extra birthday older
and can go to princess school right now!
Place: The Great Hall
Time: 4 o'clock tomorrow
Dress: A perfect pretty party frock, please!

"A perfect pretty party frock?" Haggle scratched his head. "I don't think I have one of those," he said.

"All the birthday guests in my storybooks wear perfect pretty party frocks," Pip said. "That's how you can tell it's a proper perfect princess party. Next, I need a unicorn."

"A unicorn?" gasped Haggle.

"A proper princess always arrives at her perfect party on a unicorn," Pip said, and off she ran.

Chapter Four

At teatime the next day the Great Hall was full of noise and laughter.

Haggle the herdsman was there . . . with a big pink bow in his beard.

The king was there, too. And all his hairy
warriors.

Wise Gogo was dozing under the table. Canker the cook was handing out teacups.

Everyone looked a bit embarrassed. But they were all wearing pretty party frocks, just as they had been told.

"You have to obey a proper pink party invitation from a princess," blushed Haggle.

"I know," agreed Canker, straightening his frilly pink apron strings.

"But where is Princess Pip?" said the king.
"After all, it's her party!"

Suddenly the royal musician squeezed his
bagpipes.

There was a sound like a squealing piglet and . . .

"All hail the birthday girl," cried the hairy
warriors.

Princess Pip rode into the Great Hall.

She hadn't been able to find a unicorn – the best she could manage was a yak with a broomstick tied to the top of his head.

But Pip didn't mind.

The cake wasn't covered in icing. And it was shaped like a yak, of course.

But Pip didn't mind. She blew out the wobbly candles in one big puff.

The royal musician only knew yak-herding
songs and couldn't play the tune to Happy
Birthday.

But Pip didn't mind that either.

"It's just perfect!" she cried.

And everyone agreed it was a party any proper princess could be proud of!

They played plenty of perfectly silly party games, like tie the ribbon on the yak . . . and who could make the rudest sound by blowing on the bagpipes.

"Three cheers for our perfect princess,"
everybody cried.

And when the cake had been eaten and the games were over, the king took Pip by the hand.

"I know you had an extra birthday party today," he said. "But you're still not old enough to go to princess school, I'm afraid. You'll have to have a few more birthdays before you're ready for that."

"More birthdays? How perfect," grinned Pip.
"My next party shall be a magnificent ball."
"When will it be?" gulped the king.

"Tomorrow, of course!"cried Pip. "Don't forget to practise your dancing and wear your very best ballgowns, everyone!"

Then she curtsied politely, just like a proper perfect princess would.